Kevin
In Between

Kevin In Between

Patricia Lees

Illustrated by
Dana Welch

NIMBUS
PUBLISHING

Nimbus Publishing Limited
P.O. Box 9301, Station A
Halifax, N.S.
B3K 5N5

Design Editor: Kathy Kaulbach
Project Editor: Alexa Thompson

Nimbus Publishing Limited gratefully acknowledges the support of the Council of Maritime Premiers and the Department of Communications.

Canadian Cataloguing in Publication Data

Lees, Patricia.

Kevin in between

(New Waves)

ISBN 0-921054-73-4

I. Welch, Dana.   III. Title.   III.   Series.

PS8573.E33K48 1991   jC813'.54   C90-097702-7
PZ7.L43Ke 1991

Printed and bound in Canada

Contents

1
The Old Stone Bridge

When Kevin was ten years old, he and the bicycle he was riding collided with a large oil truck. For Kevin, everything went blank.

After a while he became aware again but could not understand why there was nothing around him. He thought perhaps he might be dead. "But they told me," he said, to no one in particular, because there was no one to say it to, "that heaven would be full of angels and harps. There should be fountains, and houses that look like old Mrs. Conway's down the street—with columns and curly carving around the windows. All I can see is a big, empty space. Where *is* everything?"

He floated in space for what seemed a very long time. It was hard to judge how long, of course, for there were no clocks, or school bells, or dinner times, or even sunrises. It was not unpleasant, just a trifle unsettling and, eventually, rather dull. He began to find it tiresome that there was no one to talk to; he had so many questions and there was nobody to answer them.

Kevin's only experience of death had been a favorite uncle who had died two years earlier. Uncle Gregory had been a gentle and imaginative person, with wavy, fair hair and amused blue eyes. He was a bit of an artist too, and would draw scenes on the backs of old envelopes for his nephew. Kevin's favorite had been one they called the "The Old Stone Bridge," and he never tired of watching his uncle draw it. There would be a little stream running through a grassy meadow, with a few trees around, a cottage in the background and, in the centre of the sketch, an old stone bridge across the stream. They used to make up stories about what happened in the scene and sometimes his uncle would put in strange animals and little people.

The boy started to think about Uncle Gregory and, suddenly, the mist which had surrounded him began to part as if blown away by the breeze and he saw the Old Stone Bridge, the stream and the trees. Across the bridge strode his uncle.

"Uncle Gregory, am I glad to see *you*," Kevin shouted as he ran toward him. "How did you know where to find me?"

His uncle smiled and said, "I can't answer that question right now. In a little while, after you have got used to it here, I'll be able to tell you. Right now you wouldn't understand. In the meantime, what would you like to do?"

"Well," answered Kevin, "I suppose I should be hungry because I was on my way home for supper when I hit that truck. Just the same, I don't feel much like eating. But I would like to explore this place."

So they set off together, back across the bridge and up the grassy bank, through the trees, which looked very much the same as the trees which grew in Kevin's garden, and up the path to the cottage.

Inside, everything seemed familiar. "I've been here before," said Kevin.

"Yes," his uncle replied, "I expect you have."

The rooms were like the ones he had seen in an old house when he had been on holiday with his parents. They had gone to Sherbrooke Village, an historical restoration where the homes were the same as those built by settlers two hundred years before. "How odd," said Kevin, "that the cottage should be so very much the same as those old houses."

His uncle seemed to be amused. "Not really," he said.

When Kevin looked out of the windows he could see green fields and farmland with horses and cows, and a road winding and dipping through the hills. He began to think about his bicycle and how great it would be to go skimming along the road.

The next moment there he was, pedalling furiously, just the way he used to, enjoying the feeling of the wind rushing through his hair and up his nose, and of his legs pumping up and down. "Oh boy," he yelled, "this is terrific!"

But after a time he started to feel very much alone again as now his uncle was nowhere in sight. Kevin didn't like the idea of getting lost in this strange place. He thought, "I wish Uncle Gregory was here"—then, around the next bend, there he was, waiting.

"How did you get here ahead of me?" Kevin gasped.

"That's a trick you'll discover before too long, but you'll have to find it out for yourself," his uncle replied.

They left the bicycle under a big oak tree and strolled along, hand in hand. Kevin was so full of questions that he didn't know what to ask first. Shyly and rather tentatively, he asked, "Do you think that I might be dead?"

"Really can't tell you," his uncle replied. "You may be, but then again, you may not."

Suddenly, Kevin felt very depressed. He wanted a real, concrete kind of answer, not the sort of riddle his uncle was giving him. In fact he was getting rather tired of his uncle's riddles.

"I want to know where I am," he said rather

fiercely, standing in the middle of the road and refusing to go on.

Uncle Gregory looked at him seriously and then said kindly, "You're wherever you want to be, Kevin."

The boy kicked at a stone and stuffed his clenched hands into his pockets. "I don't understand," he muttered miserably. He was very close to tears.

"Neither did I at first," his uncle admitted. "But it will come to you if you keep an open mind and don't let yourself get too unhappy about it."

"Well, I am unhappy," Kevin blurted out. In a moment he was experiencing the dreadful misery he'd felt when he had been ill with chicken pox and missed going to summer camp. He had the same awful lump in his throat, the prickly eyes, the same feeling of frustration and disappointment—and the same fury at not being able to control things.

"Oh, I hate it here," he cried. "I want to go back."

He thought longingly of his own comfortable

room—the small boat he had been constructing from a kit, the comics piled untidily on the shelf, his cassette player, his own bed, even his school books.

In an instant all these things surrounded him. He recognized every familiar object with joy—the blue and orange cover on the bed, the box of miniature cars that he hadn't played with for months, even the chewed slipper that his dog Bosun had left under the armchair. The security of home was folded around him like a warm blanket.

"I think I'll just stay here for a bit," he said, "until I get more used to things."

"That's perfectly all right," Uncle Gregory said, "I'll be around when you think of me again."

Kevin climbed onto his bed and, shoving his feet under the covers, curled up into a ball. He was so happy to be back but, as he lay there, he began to turn over in his mind the things that had happened to him since he had collided with the truck—his uncle appearing like that, the sketch coming to life, the cottage he'd seen before, his bicycle ride through the country lanes. And now, he was back here in his own room again. His curiosity was getting the better of him and he started to wonder if he hadn't abandoned his strange adventure too soon.

He had always been a thoughtful child who had liked to work out puzzles, so he found the answers coming to him more easily than he expected.

His uncle's last words had been, "I'll be around when you think of me again."

Kevin sat bolt upright on the bed. He thought hard about his uncle and there he was, sitting in the armchair, smiling approvingly.

"I believe you've got the hang of it," he said.

"I'm just beginning to understand, "Kevin said slowly. "Is it possible that I'm inventing my own world using everything that's ever happened to me until now?"

"That's it!" his uncle said happily. "Once you know that, you can really begin to enjoy yourself. There's no need to be depressed any more."

Kevin nodded. He took one last look around his old bedroom before thinking himself into the circus. He'd always loved circuses.

2
Intermission

The truck driver was overcome with grief. "I never saw the kid," he moaned, as he knelt beside Kevin's limp body. "He shot out of that side street, turning straight into me. I never even saw him coming."

It was true. Kevin must have been thinking about how fast he could go on his bike and had obviously forgotten that the road ahead was a busy one. The truck driver had no chance at all to brake. He'd caught sight of the boy out of the corner of his eye just before the collision and swerved wildly to avoid him—but in vain. Kevin hit the rear of the truck head on.

Within minutes the police were on the scene. Then the ambulance came, with siren blaring, to take Kevin to the hospital. There he was rushed straight into the operating room where the medical team worked valiantly to bring him back to consciousness.

His parents were contacted and, filled with fear, they arrived at his bedside to be met by the doctor who looked very grave indeed.

"Your little boy is in serious condition," she told them. "We've done all we can for him but he's in a deep coma and may stay like this for days, maybe even weeks. He has a very severe concussion."

Kevin's mom and dad clung together, as the doctor said kindly, "You mustn't lose hope. We can never tell exactly how injuries like this will affect someone. Kevin is a strong lad and may well come round in a day or so and be perfectly all right. But," she warned, "you must also be prepared for a long wait. Just keep hoping and stay with him as much as you possibly can. It may help if you talk to him, even if he doesn't answer."

So it was that either Kevin's mother or father were by his bed almost all the time, taking turns to watch over him. They brought along some of his toys and pinned his uncle's picture, "The Old Stone Bridge," above his bed. His mom would gently stroke his hand and talk to him quietly, hoping for some sign of recovery. His dad read stories to him from his favorite books, thinking that somehow he might get through to his son.

The days dragged by and still Kevin lay unconscious. He looked quite peaceful, as though he were asleep, but there was no movement. Tubes had been inserted up his nose to help him breath more easily, and into a vein in his arm to provide nourishment. His breathing, although shallow, was steady, but he was quite passive.

One evening when his father was reading to him about the circus, the boy stirred a little and seemed to respond just a tiny bit. He even gave a flicker of a smile but then lay still again, a pale, pathetic little lad in constant danger of slipping away for ever.

3
Taking Charge

The smell of sawdust was strong in Kevin's nose as he watched the bareback riders on their ponies. Round the ring they raced, the acrobats balancing first on one leg, then on the other. Some even stood on their hands on the ponies' backs as they cantered around.

Then the clowns came on with their silly, painted faces and loose, baggy pants. With them were the chimpanzees dressed in velvet jackets and little round hats. They carried buckets of water and sloshed them over the clowns who fell down and slid about helplessly in the puddles while Kevin was equally helpless with laughter.

A roll of drums announced the trapeze artists who trouped in wearing dazzling, white costumes trimmed with sequins. They seemed just as much at home in the air as eagles, and their daring feats took the boy's breath away. These were all his favorite circus acts and he was enjoying himself hugely.

He began to wonder idly how the chimpanzees would manage on the high wire. In a flash they were up there, gingerly walking along the wire and then flinging themselves on to the trapeze, chattering and squealing and tying themselves into knots. They were almost better than the human acrobats, Kevin thought. He found that by using his imagination he could rearrange all the circus performers and animals to suit his own liking. He soon had the bareback riders sloshing water all over each other and the clowns riding the ponies. It was tremendous fun.

When he got tired of doing that, he looked around for Uncle Gregory. This time he wasn't in the least surprised to find him sitting in the next seat. He was beginning to get used to his uncle being on hand whenever he needed him.

"That was great," Kevin said, "and it was neat being able to change things around like that. It made me feel almost as though I was in charge."

"That's just what you are," his uncle replied. "You've discovered already that you can make up your own adventures out of things that you've seen and done before. You'll enjoy it, but there's more to it than that, you know," he added mysteriously.

Kevin wasn't really listening. He was too thrilled with his new ability to recreate all the good things that had happened to him before the accident.

It wasn't too long before another idea occurred to him. He'd go sailing! No sooner had he started to think about it than he was bobbing along on the waves in a sturdy little sailboat. The lovely bay where he found himself was just like the place where he'd spent summer holidays by the sea with his parents. His father had built him a small sailboat and Kevin had learned to handle it so well that on calm days, when the breeze was gentle, he was allowed to take it out by himself. He was so proud the first few times he'd sailed the little craft single-handedly. Soon he wanted to take it out when the wind was strong enough to make sailing really exciting, but his parents wouldn't allow it. He got very sulky about that. Now was his chance to sail the way he had always longed to, fast and furiously before a strong wind.

Kevin thought hard about the wind, which at the moment was merely rippling the water in a playful way. Soon it picked up and the boat began to scud along nicely. Kevin was delighted. "This is more like it," he shouted. He started to sing, "The wind is blowing, look how I'm going and there's nobody no-ing."

His enthusiasm grew with the wind and he hardly noticed how fast he was moving until an extra strong gust suddenly went screaming through the rigging, almost tearing the sail off and flattening the craft on its beam.

The sky had darkened and the waves were

mounting higher. Instead of being a sparkling blue the water now turned dark and turbulent, with flecks of white froth spinning off into the air. The sea had an evil character all its own and Kevin's mild alarm turned to real fear. Rain fell in torrents; purple clouds bruised the sky, looming over the bay like huge, menacing monsters. The little boat, out of control now, was performing a crazy dance, and Kevin, confused and terrified, cowered in the bottom of it.

He had got exactly what he wished for and he didn't like it!

The rain lashed him and the shrieking wind tore at his jacket. He was cold and wet and breathless and very sorry that he had called up such a storm.

In desperation he thought of his Uncle Gregory, who immediately appeared in the boat beside him. "You've got to take control again, Kevin," he shouted over the wind. "I can't help you. You have to do it yourself."

"Oh, what *can* I do?" Kevin wailed, scared out of his wits.

"Take charge," his uncle repeated, cupping his hands around his mouth to make himself heard. Then he disappeared.

Kevin, clinging to the side of the boat with all his strength, his teeth chattering with cold and fear, could hardly get his thoughts in order. With a great effort he took a grip on himself and said, "I got myself into this mess and now I'm obviously expected to get myself out of it. But how?"

Then it came to him. "I suppose I must *imagine* myself out of it." That was a pretty hard thing to do in a lurching boat with the wind howling in his ears and water running down his neck, but he concentrated with all his might on sunny skies, calm seas and a gentle breeze. As he kept his thoughts firmly on that peaceful scene, he found the wind was gradually dropping. Soon the storm clouds rolled away and the sun shone again on the sparkling blue sea as though the storm had never been.

Kevin brought the little craft to shore, tied it up at a breakwater and flung himself down on

the sand, panting and puffing and still shaking from his adventure.

His uncle was sitting on a rock, grinning at him. "That'll teach you to *think* before you think, if you get my meaning," he laughed. "You can't be careless with your thoughts you know. You have to be more responsible than that. In fact you'll find you have more responsibility here than you ever had before."

"Oh dear," Kevin said ruefully, "there's an awful lot to learn here. I thought I'd have finished with lessons and all that sort of thing. I thought it would all be easy—that I'd be happy all the time and everything would be just great."

"Oh, indeed no," said Uncle Gregory. "It's a different kind of school here. In some ways you'll find it much harder because you have a lot more freedom now. You have to expect the unexpected here," the older man went on, "but you'll find it more rewarding when you've learned a bit more self control. It takes practice though, rather like learning to ride your bicycle. You need to strike a balance."

The boy looked at his uncle. "I'm sure glad I've got you to talk to," he said. "It really is a big help."

"Yes, well, it doesn't hurt to have a few pointers when you first arrive," his uncle smiled.

4
The Pony Lesson

Kevin was a quick learner, especially if something really interested him. Of course, this didn't mean that he was excellent in everything, in fact his school reports were quite mediocre: "Kevin has a good mind and learns well if only he would apply himself." If he was not particularly interested in a subject he more or less ignored it. This was frustrating for his teachers who knew he could do better and for his parents who wanted him do well.

But here, in these new and fascinating surroundings, Kevin was eager to learn. He absorbed Uncle Gregory's lessons like a young seal swallowing fish.

When he came to think about it, his uncle didn't actually *tell* him very much. He just hinted at things and then let him find out for himself. Kevin was beginning to think that this was probably the very best way for anyone to learn because it was such fun. He soon started to treat his vivid imagination with care, knowing that in this place his thoughts brought results. It seemed that anything he imagined could come true here. "If only it could have been like this in the real world," he sighed, "what a terrific time I would have had."

He told his uncle that he wished he had been able to make his dreams come true before his accident.

"That may be what you think now," his uncle replied, "but it's not necessarily a good thing to always get what you wish for. Would you really have liked to have been at a circus whenever you imagined it? You'd have missed all the fun of waiting for the circus to come."

"I guess so," Kevin answered doubtfully, "but I still think it would be great to have everything you want just by thinking about it."

"You mean like the circus and the sailing?" his uncle asked.

"No, I mean *things* that I'd like to have," Kevin explained. "Things I could play with and keep—not just experiences."

"Want to try it?"

"Oh, yes!" Kevin shouted, jumping up and down. "I'd love that."

He screwed up his eyes, imagining hard a brand new bike with twelve speeds, a whole table full of banana splits, the latest CD player with a stack of discs six feet high, an astronaut's outfit, the chemistry set he'd wanted but wasn't allowed to have at home because it was too dangerous, and, the thing he wanted most of all, a pony of his own.

It was the pony that brought him to his senses. However hard he tried he simply couldn't ride it. In no time at all he had tired of the bicycle and was feeling queasy after too many banana splits. He was deafened by the CD player and was bored with pretending to be an astronaut (after all, he'd already travelled further than any astronaut, hadn't he?). The chemistry set really was too complicated. All that was left was the pony.

Why couldn't he ride it? He wanted to so much. But each time he approached the shaggy little animal he found he could get no farther than putting his hand on its back. Then he seemed to freeze.

The pony was friendly enough. It looked at him with large, brown eyes, making snuffling noises through its soft nose. Kevin talked to it and even gave it a name—Pit—although he couldn't understand why he'd given it such a *funny* name. It didn't make much sense, but sounded right somehow. The animal seemed to know him and its rough mane felt familiar under his hand, but just the same, as soon as he thought of actually riding Pit his mind went blank and there was nothing he could do about it.

In sheer exasperation Kevin called to Uncle Gregory for help.

"Hello there. What's up?" his uncle asked, sitting astride the pony with a little smirk on his lips.

"Oh, how is it you can get on the pony and I can't?" Kevin was almost in a temper by now. "I've been trying and trying and I can't seem to manage it."

"If you remember," his uncle said, "when you were about seven, your mother offered to let you have riding lessons and you said you didn't want to learn."

"Yes, I know," the boy replied sulkily, "but that was then and this is now, and I feel differently about it. I'd just *love* to ride this pony. It would be new and difficult and I'm so bored with all the other things I thought of."

"Well, now, I see you've learned two lessons at once, which is pretty clever of you."

"What lessons?" Kevin asked, becoming curious in spite of himself.

"Lesson number one," Uncle Gregory said, holding up a finger, "you get bored when things come to you too easily. And lesson number two," holding up a second finger, "if you didn't take the trouble to try to learn a skill when you had the chance, then you can't use it here."

"Oh, no!" wailed Kevin, "That means I'll never be able to ride a pony."

"Yes, you will, one day," Uncle Gregory said mysteriously, "but that's another story."

5
A Friendly Reunion

Much as Kevin loved and respected his uncle he began to feel the need for a companion his own age. He was very much aware of the fact that Uncle Gregory was the only other person he had seen so far in this new place. There was Pit of course, but he was just a pony.

He didn't want to hurt the older man's feelings, but eventually he had to mention his problem. They were sitting on the shore close to where Kevin had landed his boat after the storm. The tide was out and the sand was hard and smooth.

Kevin said, "Would you mind drawing some pictures for me, the way you used to?"

Uncle Gregory found a sharp piece of

seashell and started to draw their favorite, "The Old Stone Bridge."

"No, not that," Kevin said quickly, seeing his chance to bring up a delicate subject tactfully. "Draw me some people."

His uncle gave him a look. Then, slowly, he sketched a number of Kevin's school friends.

The boy swallowed hard. "I sure would like to see them again," he murmured sadly. "It's not that I don't enjoy being with you, but it's...."

"I understand," his uncle broke in kindly. "It's time you had some company of your own age. Now, this is a little difficult in your case because you've been separated from your friends and believe that you don't know anyone here except me. It's hard for you to figure out, but, in fact, you have lots of friends here. You just don't know you know them yet. So, to make things easier for yourself why not meet one of your old friends from home?"

"Oh, could that really happen?" Kevin asked laughingly. "How could it be possible?"

"Well, it's done through dreams. You choose

which friend you'd like to see again and then that friend will meet you in a dream."

"I think I'd like to see Milly again," Kevin said. Milly was a girl who lived two doors down on his street. She was a year older and a very interesting young person, full of ideas for games and always ready for a new adventure. Kevin thought she had more guts than his other friends. She was also very understanding and he knew it would be wonderful to talk to her about his new situation. He even felt a small sense of triumph because he was doing something that she hadn't done.

The two friends were always playing "one-upmanship" games, each trying to outdo the other. This often got them into trouble. Kevin had a good sense of balance and had no difficulty riding his bike with "no hands." Milly, who was hopelessly uncoordinated, tried to copy him and fell right into a patch of gravel, scratching her hands and knees horribly. Her mother had been quite exasperated with her.

Milly was a strong swimmer and Kevin had

very nearly drowned one day when she swam far out into the lake and he had tried to keep up. Luckily, she had looked behind and, seeing him floundering in the water, had raced back to rescue him. They both kept quiet about this experience knowing there would be trouble if anyone found out.

Kevin turned to his uncle. "Could you arrange for me to meet Milly in a dream?" he asked.

"I don't have to arrange anything," Uncle Gregory replied. "You can do it for yourself if you just concentrate. I'm sure Milly will meet you half way."

6
Intermission

That evening Milly went to bed earlier than usual. "Don't know why I'm so tired," she told her mother, "but I sure could use a good night's sleep."

As she snuggled down under the covers she thought about Kevin. She was very fond of her young friend and the accident had shaken her up more than she would admit. Milly was the kind of girl who kept most of her important feelings to herself and so no one had guessed just how close she felt to Kevin. "In fact," she mumbled, as she was drifting off to sleep, "I feel as though he were right here, somehow."

In the morning, she broke her rule about keeping quiet about what she considered her private life. She told her mother, "I had the strangest dream about Kevin last night. I dreamed we were walking along a beautiful beach together and talking about him being in some strange, new place and what it was like there."

Her mother looked alarmed. "Milly, dear," she said, "you've just been letting that awful accident prey on your mind. I know how much you like Kevin, but you must try not to worry. It's not good for you to dwell on things like that."

Milly shrugged and gave her mother an odd look. Why would grown up people never talk about the things that were really important, she wondered? She resolved to go on keeping her thoughts to herself in future. She knew her dream was more than just something "preying on her mind" but it was impossible to explain.

"I won't talk about it any more," she decided. But the next night she fell asleep with Kevin again on her mind and, once more, the two friends met.

As they strolled along the beach Kevin was saying, "It's like this, you see. Any experience

you've had can be used while you're here. If you've chosen before *not* to do something then you lose out here—that's why I can't ride Pit. Uncle Gregory says I may be able to one day." He patted the pony which had taken to following him about like a dog.

Milly answered, "I think I know that already. I find it awfully hard *not* to do new things, and I'm always getting into trouble at home for being what Mom calls reckless—but I can't seem to help myself."

"I shouldn't worry about that if I were you,"

said Kevin, unconsciously copying his uncle's way of talking.

Then he added, "There's another thing I've discovered here. Once you've owned something it's yours for ever. I mean you don't have to hang on to things. If you have a special toy you can quite easily give it away, because it will always be yours. You only have to think about it to have it again."

"And it also becomes the other person's too," Milly said quickly, carrying the idea forward. "I gave my doll house away to my little cousin last year. She really loves it. But I still feel it belongs to me because I had it for so long it almost seems like a part of me."

"Yes, and your cousin would feel the same way if *she* gave it away," Kevin laughed, "because she'd owned it for a while."

"I kind of like that idea, although Mom gets mad when I give things away. I don't think she'd understand if I explained, though."

"Oh, she'll probably understand one day," her friend replied sagely, full of his newly found insights.

Milly was very quiet for several minutes. She bent down and picked up a piece of seaweed. Shredding it with her fingers, she said thoughtfully, "You know, I don't think I'd mind being here one bit. Seems to me you're having a very interesting time of it."

"Well, yes and no." (*When* would Kevin stop copying his uncle?) "I still wish I'd learned to ride a pony when I had the chance."

"Oh, that old pony of yours!" said Milly impatiently. "Is that all you can think about?"

"At the moment, yes," Kevin replied haughtily, and removed himself by disappearing into a passing cloud and coming down again somewhere else in a shower of rain. Pit galloped off after him, whinnying anxiously.

Milly woke up suddenly. "That was so *real*," she whispered to herself. "I'm sure Kevin is all right."

At breakfast she asked her mother if she could sit by Kevin's bed at the hospital after school to watch over him. "It would give his parents a rest," she said, "and I promise I will be very quiet."

Her mother wasn't sure that was a good idea. Milly's father had left several years before, and she'd been faced with all the unhappiness of a divorce. She felt that it wasn't easy bringing up a child on her own and she worried about Milly a great deal.

"You're taking this whole thing so much to heart," she said. "You haven't been yourself since Kevin had the accident and it's upsetting you."

But Milly pleaded so hard that eventually her mother said she could go providing Kevin's parents agreed. They did, gratefully, for they were both weary and badly in need of a few hours to themselves. As there was a limit to the number of friends they could ask to spend a regular time at the hospital each day, Milly's offer was more than welcome. So, after school, Milly went straight to Kevin's bedside and took over for an hour or two.

Her young friend never responded to her whispered conversations. But at night, when

Milly was home in bed, the two of them would meet in the world of dreams until Kevin began to realize that he was interfering too much in Milly's life. He was distracting her from what she should be doing and filling her head with so many unusual ideas that she was finding it hard to concentrate on everyday events.

Uncle Gregory advised Kevin, "I think it's time you let Milly go. You're confusing her, you know."

"I guess so," the boy admitted reluctantly. "I can see that. I expect she isn't sure which life is real and which is a dream. And I keep feeding her so many odd ideas that other people will start thinking she is weird or something! I'll be awfully sorry not to meet her for a while, but I suppose it is not really fair. I'll just have to wait."

His uncle looked at him proudly. "You've come a long way since you arrived, Kevin," he said. "I think it's time now for you to meet those other friends I told you about—the ones I said you didn't know you knew."

7
Edgar

The boy stood awkwardly, for one leg had been taken off at the knee. He had a crutch made from a rough piece of wood. His dark, curly hair was matted and dirty and his clothes were so patched and mended that it was hard to tell what the original garments had been like.

Kevin stared at the lad. He knew that face— the defiant green eyes, the small mouth compressed into a hard line, the thin arms as strong as steel.

A name swam dimly into his memory, then slid away again as he tried to catch it, like a ghostly water snake.

Suddenly it was there. "Edgar," he cried, leaping forward and throwing his arms around the urchin. Edgar laughed and, as his face lighted up, his body seemed to become whole again. "Sorry about the missing leg," he said cheerfully, "but I knew that was the only way you'd recognize me."

"Oh, Edgar," Kevin breathed, "how could I have forgotten you?"

"Well, you did, at least for a while," his friend replied. "And, by the way, Alfred, you've changed quite a bit yourself. You look much too clean and tidy for my memory."

Kevin took a step back. "Why did you call me Alfred?" he muttered cautiously. "My name is Kevin."

"Oh, beg your pardon, I'm sure," Edgar replied, with a crooked grin. "Kevin is your latest name, but you were Alf when I knew you."

Kevin was puzzled. "I suppose I should understand, but just now I'm rather full of being me and I can't honestly see where Alfred comes into it."

"Let me jog your memory," Edgar suggested. "Think back—many children like us, aged ten or eleven, were sent to work in the mines. We were in the North of England and Victoria was Queen. We were friends then—working together in the same mine. That's where I lost my leg, when there was an underground explosion."

Memories came flooding back until Kevin thought he might faint with the shock. The sun disappeared and he found himself, choking with coal dust, in a long, dark, narrow tunnel. It was unbearably hot and stuffy and he felt as though he had not breathed real air since he'd left home at five o'clock that morning. Sweat was running into his eyes, making it even harder to see anything in the dim light. But he could feel. The uneven ground under his feet sloped upwards at a slight angle. Under his left hand he felt the rough mane of the pit pony that was hauling coal to the surface. The heavy load, piled on a wooden wagon which ran on steel rails like a train, was almost too much for the willing little beast. Alfred's heart bled for the creature.

He felt just as sorry for the pony as he felt for himself and he wished they could both leave this place for ever and spend their days in green meadows in the clean air.

The pony and his friend, Edgar, made his dreadful life just bearable. He didn't think he could manage if anything happened to either of them. His devotion to the pony had already got him into trouble with the foreman, a hard-faced man who accused him of "spoiling the dumb thing." Once he had caught Alfred offering it an apple—such a luxury! And another time he had stopped the boy from trying to clamber onto the animal's back for a free ride to the pithead.

"Look 'ere," the foreman said roughly, "this ain't no riding school you know. If I catch you tryin' to ride that beast again, you'll get kicked out. Understand?"

Alfred's job was to guide the pony out of the mine and return with it below ground to where the coal was being cut. Load after load was delivered to the surface in this way and if the quota wasn't met, the boy knew he'd likely lose his job. Although he hated the work passionately, his family was so poor that he knew his parents would never manage without the small sum he brought home each week.

His friend Edgar had an even harder job. As he was older and stronger he worked at the pitface cutting out slabs of coal—crouched hour after hour in a low, cramped space. It was dangerous work; the mine's owner had no thought for the safety of his workers.

Today was a bad day. The miners were grumbling that the air below was even worse than usual. But the foreman wouldn't listen and told them they were "just lazy louts, lookin' for sympathy." He sneered at them, "There's lots more would jump at your jobs any time you want to quit." He knew very well that the poor wretches would starve if they were out of work.

Alfred was at the pithead when he heard a roar like the sound of a huge waterfall … then a series of ominous rumbles … then silence.

When they started to bring out the dead and injured, Alfred was distraught. He could think only of Edgar. Presently he saw his young friend, white and unconscious, but still breathing, being carried out by two men. He tried to run over to him, but was held back by one of the miners. "Stay here, lad," the older man said. "Your friend is in pretty bad shape."

Alfred, his grimy face streaked with tears, asked, "Is he going to die?"

"We don't know, lad," the miner told him. "But even if he lives, he's never going to walk right again. He got trapped under a fall of rock that crushed his leg. They'll have to take it off."

Alfred flinched as though he'd been struck. Having a limb cut off was a terrible thing, almost worse than dying. There would be nothing to help the pain except a mug of raw rum. He could only pray that Edgar would remain unconscious.

"Oh, Edgar, I remember everything—it was *awful*!" Kevin cried.

"I know," his friend said solemnly, waiting for Kevin to calm down. "It seemed dreadful at the time. But when you look back you can see that some good came of it."

"There was *nothing* good about it," Kevin replied indignantly. "It was foul working underground. We were always tired and hungry—and poor!"

"But just think," Edgar insisted. "Remember, in spite of the misery, we never lacked the important things of life. We always had our friends and the love of our families. Also, because of all those years I spent underground, the things of nature—the trees, birds and flowers—were always wonderful to me. In fact, after I lost my leg, I started sketching—and I made some money by selling my pictures at local fairs. So," he concluded, "you can't say it was *all* bad."

The two boys spent long hours talking about their times together. "It was a friendship that lasted all our lives," Kevin said, "and, when you died, I never forgot you."

"Yes, you did," Edgar reminded him. "You forgot me when you became Kevin."

"I suppose so," Kevin admitted rather

sheepishly. "But I couldn't help that. I think I must have always remembered some things from that time, because, as Kevin, I have a horrible fear of being underground. When other kids go exploring caves or the cellar of an abandoned house, I won't go. Do you suppose it's because of those days in the mine when I was Alf?"

"Could be," his friend told him, "especially as that wasn't so long ago. But other experiences you've had go back much further and they'd probably seem very vague to you. That is, until you came here for your In-Between lessons."

"I guess I see what you mean," Kevin mused, "I often have odd feelings about all sorts of things I can't explain—hating dark caves, for instance, and the way I love the circus, almost as though I was part of it."

The friends lay on their backs under the trees that Edgar loved so much, listening to the birds. The pony, Pit, was nearby, contentedly cropping the grass. Kevin was watching him idly when he realized why he had given the creature such a funny name. "He's a pit pony!" he yelled, startling Edgar who had almost drifted off to sleep.

"Well, aren't you the clever one," Edgar chuckled. As Kevin explained how he had been unable to ride Pit, his friend jumped up and held out his hand. "Come on now," he said. "You're getting so smart it's time for you to meet another of your old friends—*really* old this time!"

8
Intermission

Milly was sitting by Kevin's bedside, gazing at him intently, searching for some little movement. A few moments ago she thought he had tried to clench his fists, as though something was upsetting him. "I wonder what's going on in his mind?" she asked herself, for she was quite convinced that he was still aware in some way.

She was disappointed that her dreams of Kevin had ended a few nights ago. Although they had helped to make her feel better about her friend, she had been getting into trouble at school for daydreaming in class.

"What's come over you Milly?" her teacher had asked gently. "Your mind seems to be far away. I know you're worried and upset about

Kevin, but wasting your time in class is not going to help him.

Milly smiled ruefully. It was so true!

However, since the dreams had ended she found she could concentrate on her lessons again. "I don't think I could have gone on having a foot in each world," Milly thought.

She had brought some of her school books with her so that she wouldn't fall behind with her homework. "I don't want them to stop me coming here because I'm not getting my assignments in on time," she said to herself.

The book she was reading was about Ancient Greece and the origin of the Olympic games. "What wonderful athletes they must have been!" she thought. Unfortunately, the book was rather dull, and Milly's attention began to wander. All at once there was a curious roaring in her ears and a feeling of excitement mixed with sadness. She noticed Kevin's feet were flexing under the covers, almost as if he was trying to run. Then he was still once more. The roaring faded and Milly went back to her book, confused and a little scared.

9
The Bull Leaper

The bull was massive. Although it was on the far side of the ring, Kevin could hear the animal breathing—air flowing in and out of its great lungs like a wind that starts to blow just before a storm breaks.

The amphitheatre was packed with people, all silent now as they watched the youth and the fierce, black bull facing each other. The contrast between the two was frightening. The boy was so slender and graceful—the bull primitive, hairy and enraged.

Kevin felt tense and, at the same time, light-headed. This was to be his first public performance; the daring feat of bull-leaping was what he had been trained for since he was a child. Whatever happened he must not disgrace himself, or his teammate, the girl Megara, who stood quietly behind the bull keeping well out of sight.

The boy stood watching the animal through narrowed eyes. Then he started to sway from side to side, engaging the beast's attention. It snorted, and pawed the ground. Then it lunged, thundering across the ring toward Kevin who raised himself high on his toes and ran forward. When it seemed as though the two must meet head on with killing impact, the boy sprang lightly into the air and, grasping the bull's horns, twisted himself over its back and somersaulted onto the sand at the side of the waiting girl. She steadied him as he dropped to his feet.

The crowd exploded. Flowers and garlands were thrown into the ring as the people roared their approval, calling Kevin by name.

"Darius! Darius!" they shouted. Megara whispered in his ear, "Darius, you did it! What a triumph!"

Kevin, realizing in a flash that he was Darius,

gave her arm a squeeze before leaving her side to walk to the center of the ring where he took bow after bow. The great bull had been captured and taken away.

Smiling proudly, the dark, slim-waisted youth revelled in the applause. Bull leaping was the most dangerous and popular sport in Crete and any athlete who became an accomplished leaper was a national hero.

Presently the crowd, overcome with admiration and enthusiasm for their idol, clambered over the partition and spilled into the ring. Carrying Darius shoulder high, they paraded around the amphitheatre, singing and chanting his name. The court poets hurriedly began to rack their brains for the right words to describe the event. Heroes must always be celebrated in verse and although the poetry was often a bit overblown, it was a nice compliment.

Darius, meanwhile, was glowing. He simply couldn't have enough of this adulation. "I guess I deserve it," he said to himself. "After all, I spent years learning to leap and it's not everyone who can perform a dangerous stunt like that."

Megara, who had been pushed aside by the crowd and was now some distance behind, looked wistfully at the figure of her teammate being carried off to the palace. Darius had not looked once in her direction. If he hadn't squeezed her arm after landing at her side she might have been forgiven for thinking he didn't even know she was there.

She felt hurt, although she tried to make excuses for him in her heart. She had spent just as many hours in the ring, standing by as he practised the leaps, always ready to spring to his aid if he made a slip, always there when he needed her. Her role was very important, for if Darius had fallen after leaping the bull, he needed someone there to pull him to his feet immediately, in case the maddened beast turned on him.

Megara loved Darius very much, but it was a sad kind of love for she knew his head was easily turned and there were so many beautiful girls anxious to be seen with him. And now that he'd become a hero there would be more than ever.

The crowd had reached the palace courtyard where a great banquet was to be held in honor of the games. Darius was the guest of honor! The youth, naturally accepting the fact that he was now a great hero, did not pause to reflect that if he had not succeeded in his wonderful leap the fickle crowd would soon have found someone else to carry shoulder high, to praise and flatter. In fact, Darius was unbearably swollen-headed about his success, which was a pity, since he was really a brave and hard-working athlete.

He ate and drank so much that soon he became quite befuddled and dozed contentedly in a corner of the courtyard, still surrounded by a crowd of admirers.

The scene faded gradually and Kevin found himself murmuring, "I wonder what year this would be?"

Megara answered his question, "It's twenty-five hundred years before Christ."

Kevin sat up. The palace courtyard had gone and he was sitting with a girl, and Edgar, on a hillside with fields of wild flowers and sweet smelling herbs stretched out below. The red earth had just been ploughed and seemed alight with an inner fire. Mountains reared up around them, jutting against the sky, while the sun twinkled off the green and purple sea in the distance.

"That's right," Edgar said, for all the world as though it was quite normal for him to be in Crete more than four thousand years before his own birth in Victorian England. "You became one the best bull leapers of the decade. You were very famous, although more than a bit conceited with it, I'm afraid. I thought you might enjoy that little episode again and it was a good way to get you and Megara together after all this time."

Kevin looked at the girl. Her tightly coiled hair was decorated with a fine, gold filigree. She was as slim-waisted as he and tanned brown by the hot Cretan sun. Her small, pointed chin was firm and her eyes held an honesty that was dazzling.

"When you said I was going to meet a really old friend this time," Kevin said wryly, "I thought you meant someone about eighty years old, not someone just a bit older than me."

"Well, look at it this way," Edgar grinned. "Megara's about forty-five hundred years old if you insist on being Kevin."

The girl smiled at Kevin. "I was your friend as well as your teammate. We made a very handsome couple and the crowds loved us. But I was always so afraid that the bull would get you one day."

"It didn't though, did it?" Kevin laughed.

"No," Megara admitted, "but neither did I."

"What do you mean?" Kevin asked, puzzled.

"I always loved you," the girl said, ruefully, "but you never really noticed me except when we worked together in the ring. There were many times when you nearly broke my heart."

Kevin felt a stab of remorse. How could he have hurt such an honest and beautiful girl?

Edgar was watching him, "We're often

unkind to those who love us most, you know, but our In-Between lessons help us to realize this and then we can often think of a way to make up for it another time."

"Did I ever do that for Megara?" Kevin asked hopefully. He hated the idea of her being unhappy through any fault of his. He was beginning to feel very fond of her, even if she was a few years older than he.

"No, not quite yet," Edgar replied, "but it's something you might think about. Perhaps you two could arrange to meet some time in the future and work things out."

Kevin thought to himself that he wouldn't mind that. Megara reminded him of his friend Milly. She had the same spirit of adventure, the same air of being ready for anything. He looked at her more closely. An extraordinary idea had come to his mind. He hardly dared to say anything, in case it was silly, but he had to.

"You aren't Milly too, by any chance, are you?" he asked.

Megara laughed delightedly and clapped her hands. "Yes, of course I am. I wondered if you'd guess. Milly and I are part of each other, just as you are part of Alfred and Darius."

Kevin's head was beginning to feel like a sack of chicken feathers with all these new ideas.

"What I can't understand is this," he stated. "When I was Kevin I couldn't remember being Alfred, and when I was Alfred I couldn't remember being Darius. Why not?"

"It's like being in a school play," Edgar explained. "When you're in the middle of playing a particular part it's very hard to remember the roles you've played in other years."

Kevin digested this and then came up with another poser. "If I'm Darius and Alfred and Kevin, then who am I now?"

Megara and Edgar looked at each other and giggled. "I'm afraid I'll have to give the same answer as your Uncle Gregory," Edgar said. "You're whoever you want to be."

"Oh, heavens!" Kevin said crossly. "That's much too difficult. I don't think I'll ever be able to handle it."

"Yes, you will," Megara assured him, "but you'll need a lot more practice before you feel really confident."

"Now then," Edgar chipped in with a mischievous look on his face, "before we join your uncle again, there's another surprise waiting for you."

Kevin groaned. "I think I've had enough," he said. But he didn't really mean it. He was filled with curiosity.

10
Edgar's Little Surprise

The heavy velvet skirt dragged at his legs as he tried to run. Oh, why did he have to wear these cumbersome clothes? The day was so warm he would have liked nothing better than to cast off everything and fling himself into the ornamental lake at the side of the great house. Looking around furtively, he picked up the skirt and tucked the hem into the waistband. There was no way he'd ever catch up with his brothers unless he could put on a bit more speed.

Presently, through a gap in the trees where the forest came close to the grounds of the estate, he saw the three boys with their falcons. They spotted him at the same time, and the two eldest burst out laughing. "Here comes Annette," one of them cried, "trying to keep up as usual."

Annette! Kevin looked down at himself in alarm. He was wearing the heavy, rich clothing of a wealthy young woman in 15th century France. He was a girl!

Annette's brothers waited for her to catch up.

"Pull your skirt down, you young hellion," Gaston said sharply. "You're getting too old to behave like that. You'll be twelve next birthday and that's no way for a young lady to carry herself."

Annette flushed with annoyance while she pulled the skirt hem down again. "It's all very well for you, with your breeches and boots," she retorted angrily, "but just try running in a heavy skirt."

"Well, *don't* run then," her eldest brother answered. "Girls shouldn't run—it's unseemly."

"What nonsense," Annette retorted, not in the least ready to give in. "Boys have all the fun, all the freedom, while girls have to do as they're told and be quiet and ladylike and *bored*, like me." She gave a very unladylike kick to Gaston's shin, and he, getting impatient with her, grabbed her by the shoulders and shook her.

"Just remember," he said loudly, "a girl's place is in the house. You'll never be part of a man's world so you may as well be resigned to that and behave yourself."

Jules, who was the youngest of the three boys and nearest in age to Annette, pulled her away. He was always the peacemaker between Gaston and Pierre and their high-spirited younger sister.

"It's not so very bad being a girl," he said, trying to placate her. "We boys have all the dirty work while you just sit around being waited on. You keep warm and dry while we go off to some horrible battle."

His older brothers, who had already had a taste of war against the English, nudged each other. "He'd make a grand girl himself, don't you think?" Pierre snickered.

"Oh, be quiet," Jules snapped. "It's just that I hate fighting, that's all."

"And you hate getting your hands dirty, and your feet wet," jeered Gaston. "And trapping rabbits and...."

Annette tugged at Jules's sleeve. "Come on," she urged. "Let's leave these two bullies. We'll teach your falcon some new tricks."

"He's not very good at that," Gaston called after them as they ran off. Jules, very pink in the face, was ready to burst with the unfairness of it all. He always sided with Annette because, secretly, he agreed with nearly all her rebellious ideas. It *wasn't* fair that girls weren't allowed to do the same things as boys.

"I don't feel much like teaching Sylvestre any tricks," he sighed, handing the falcon over to his sister. She would have been delighted to have a falcon of her own, but her mama had told her she should concentrate on her embroidery and not go chasing after her brothers.

Jules continued, "I know Gaston and Pierre think I'm a coward, but honestly, I don't like killing, not even a rabbit. I hate the idea of going to war. They seem to enjoy it!"

Annette loved her youngest brother, in an impatient kind of way, but she often wished he wasn't be so dreamy. "If only I could change places with you," she said enviously. "It isn't very interesting being a girl, and I'll never have the chance to do the things you can— and I'll probably have to marry someone I don't like just because Papa says so."

"Wouldn't you *mind* going to war?" Jules asked.

"No, not a bit," the girl said, thinking of all the pageantry and excitement—the sight of brilliantly coloured flags, and the thrilling sounds of blaring trumpets and clashing armour. "It beats needlework any day."

"What about the awful things that could happen, like getting an arrow in your stomach, or being clubbed over the head with a mace?" Jules shuddered.

"Oh, you don't worry about things like that unless they happen," his sister said airily.

"Well, I *do*," he replied, "and I suppose that's

what makes me different. I've got too much imagination."

"What are you going to do with your life then?" Annette asked. "In your position there's only war and hunting as far as I can see."

"I don't know yet," Jules said, "but I'll think of something. Perhaps I'll become a monk."

Annette wandered off by herself, the falcon on her arm, thinking of all the things she would do if she were a boy. "I could be an apothecary or a priest, if I didn't want to be a soldier," she told herself. "But that's not going to be the way of it—I happened to have been born a girl!"

Her steps had taken her along by the small stream that fed the ornamental lake until she came to a stone bridge.

She stopped suddenly. For some reason she didn't want to cross it. She had the strongest conviction that it would lead to a place that she wasn't ready to go to—not yet.

11
Ready to Try Again

The scene shifted as though someone had taken a pack of cards and shuffled them.

Edgar was leaning on the Old Stone Bridge, his eyes alight with amusement. "How did you like being a girl?" he asked.

Kevin felt embarrassed. "I don't think I ever really understood how difficult it can be for girls until I *was* one," he admitted.

Edgar gave him a light punch on the shoulder. "Sometimes you have to wear another person's hat to understand how they feel."

"Well, it certainly seemed very frustrating while I was Annette. And even now, five hundred years later, some things are still difficult for girls," Kevin said wonderingly.

"It all seems so silly, to make differences between people like that."

Just then they were joined by Jules and Megara and they all squatted down on the grass together, four friends who were so many more than that.

Kevin looked at the others. "I'm beginning to feel that there are bits of me in all of you somehow, and in Darius and Alfred and Annette—as though we are all part of the same jigsaw puzzle." His understanding of what was happening was something he couldn't put into words. It was more like a feeling, the sort of feeling you get when the sun is shining and your homework is all done and there are still hours in the day left to do what you want to do.

Uncle Gregory came striding along, looking as cheerful as ever. "I see young Edgar's been making himself useful," he said. "Don't know what I would have done without him, to tell you the truth." He ruffled Kevin's hair. "There are some things that are best learned from folks your own age. That's why I asked Edgar to take over at this particular point."

Kevin felt a bit huffy. "How come he knows so much more than I do?" he asked. "After all, we're the same age. Or at least we *were*," he added hurriedly.

"If you're talking about age in terms of years, I suppose you're right," his uncle admitted. "But here, experience counts for more than years and Edgar has had more experience than you. You're really quite young in the sense that you haven't done as much."

"What about Megara and Jules, then?" Kevin asked, hoping he wouldn't turn out to be the only dunce in the class.

"I'm just about where you are," Megara said, trying to spare his feelings. "Perhaps a tiny bit further ahead," she added. Sometimes her honesty could be rather a nuisance, she thought, but she didn't want to make Kevin feel stupid.

Jules said, "I'm way younger than you are in experience, so don't feel bad about not knowing too much. Imagine how I feel! And this is the first time I've been a boy," he added.

Uncle Gregory sat down beside the young people. "I expect there are other things that you find puzzling, aren't there?" he asked them.

Jules had a question. "Why are some people born disabled? It seems so unfair."

"Well, that's a real challenge for all concerned," Uncle Gregory explained, "both for those who have disabilities and for those who look after them. Those who are doing the caring must learn to look beyond the disabilities to the real person inside who needs love and respect. Disabled people don't thank you for seeing only the way they are different from other people. They'd much sooner you'd concentrate on those things they *can* do. Sometimes being in that situation allows people to grow in ways they'd never dreamed of. I expect young Edgar can tell you a thing or two about that."

"I used to get into a rage when anyone tried to stop me doing things because of my missing leg," Edgar said. "I was managing very well on crutches and soon hopped along quite fast,

but my family and friends kept doing things *for* me instead of letting me try for myself. I was so angry that they finally got the message," he grinned.

"Everything seems to be a lot clearer and makes better sense here," Megara said. "Why can't we know the answers before we come to this place? Wouldn't it make life in the real world a lot more pleasant?"

"Well, Megara," Uncle Gregory replied, "while you are here you do discover a great deal about yourself. And some of what you have discovered can be used in the real world. But you can't find out everything at once. It's like school. You can't learn everything in one year, and so you go back to school each year to learn something new."

Jules looked glum. "Does that mean that we'll keep going back and forth for ever and ever?" He liked it here and wasn't at all ready to make any changes.

"For ever and ever doesn't actually have any meaning," Uncle Gregory replied. "Time is just something man invented to make life more convenient. You know, the North American Indians think of time as a landscape. They never say, 'I didn't have enough time.' They say, 'My path didn't go that way.' But to answer your question," he went on, "if you want to find challenges, then yes, you'll go back and forth as often as you want."

He turned to his young nephew. "Do you think that being here has helped you at all?"

"Oh, yes," Kevin breathed. "In fact I'm rather anxious to try again fairly soon, if it's all right with you. I haven't had much of a chance yet. I *was* only ten when the accident happened."

All this talk about having another opportunity for life in the *real* world reminded him of his parents. He'd hardly had time to miss them since he'd been here, but now memories of his home life flooded back into his mind. He looked at his uncle through misty eyes. "It wouldn't be possible to go as Kevin again, would it?" he asked huskily. "I'm sure Mom and Dad would love to have me back."

"You've discovered for yourself how powerful thoughts can be," his uncle replied.

"And sometimes this can produce amazing results. If you truly want to go on being Kevin, and if there's someone back home who truly believes that you'll return, then it will probably work out that way. But before that happens maybe you should think about what you have learned from wearing other people's hats, as Edgar puts it."

"Well, when I was Darius I had to be courageous and discipline my body and I knew what it felt like to be famous and rich. But I was awfully vain and stuck-up, wasn't I? I suppose that's why I was Alfred later on, to learn the opposite—how it felt to be poor and humble and tired and hungry all the time. Being Annette gave me some idea of how unfair people can be to girls. I know I've often teased the girls at school, but not Milly, of course, she'd never stand for it!"

Megara hooted. "You're so right!"

Uncle Gregory stood up. "It looks as though you've learned quite a lot, young fellow. But you've only experienced a few very short episodes so far. What you have to do now is settle down and try to make sense of all the things that happened to you when you were Darius and Annette and Alfred. You'll want some peace and quiet to do that, so we're going to leave you now. I'll come back when you need me."

The man and the three young people faded away.

Kevin lay back on the sweet smelling grass, the little stream gurgling at his side, and, with the sun warm on his face, closed his eyes and dreamed a long dream.

12
A Dream Within a Dream

His lives didn't come to him one after the other. They were all mixed up, so that Darius was part of Annette, Alfred part of Kevin, as he had explained to his friends.

But there was a new dimension. It was like a slow dance, with the figures intertwining and forming wonderful patterns. It was like a great painting, with colors dark and bright, vivid and pale, making a marvelous picture. It was like a beautiful symphony, with crashing chords and soft, tender melodies, that blended into a passionate song.

Everything belonged—the good and the bad, the happy and the sad, the funny and the serious, the clever and the dull, the beautiful and the ugly, the kind and the cruel. There was a connection from rocks to rivers, from trees to toads, from pelicans to people.

Kevin stirred in his dream and finally awoke. "Uncle Gregory," he whispered.

His uncle nudged him with a toe from behind, where he was sitting on the grassy bank. Kevin jumped, and turned quickly. "I didn't know you were here already," he laughed.

"I came just as your thought was forming into words. How do you feel?"

"Absolutely marvellous," Kevin said softly. "Oh, Uncle Gregory, I had such an extraordinary dream—only it wasn't a dream really, it was more like a video."

His uncle grinned. "Really good dreams are often as much fun as seeing a movie," he said.

The boy explained, "But this wasn't like a movie exactly; it was colours and patterns and sounds all mixed together. It was the same as a video but much better than any of the videos I've ever seen before. It's really hard to describe, but it gave me this great feeling of everything being all right and having a meaning—even little tiny things that you wouldn't think were the least important."

"Yes," the older man said. "I had the same dream when I first came here. It taught me that even so-called bad things have their place. Sometimes when people have bad luck they look back on it later and realize it was good luck after all. Remember what Edgar said about losing his leg and how some good came of it? You can't always tell what's good or bad luck until a long time afterwards, and not always then."

"Yes, I remember what Edgar told me; that because he'd lost his leg, he was able to live in the fresh air and draw what he saw around him. But I still don't quite understand," Kevin said. "Surely you know bad luck is bad."

"I'll tell you an old, old story to try to make it clear to you." Kevin sat back happily. His uncle's stories were always good.

"Long ago in China," Uncle Gregory related, "there was a farmer who had a son he loved dearly. This son had a wonderful way with horses and one day he captured a beautiful wild horse and brought it home to tame it. The neighbors all came around to congratulate the farmer on his good luck. But he said to them, 'I don't know whether it's good luck or bad luck.'

"The next day, the wild horse threw the farmer's son and he broke his leg. Once more the neighbors came over, this time to say how sorry they were about his bad luck. The farmer replied, 'I don't know if it's good luck or bad luck.'

"About a week later, the authorities came to take the son away into the army but of course, he couldn't go because of the broken leg.

"So you see," Uncle Gregory explained, "it was impossible to tell at the time what was good luck and what was bad."

"That makes it much clearer," Kevin agreed, remembering the time his bike had been stolen and how upset he was. But then he recalled how much he'd enjoyed walking to school with Milly. It had really given them a chance to get to know each other better—there was always so much to talk about. He almost regretted it when his parents bought him another bike a few weeks later.

"The important thing to remember," his uncle went on, "is to live every experience as it comes along and try to get the best out of it."

Kevin looked at him. "You're starting to sound like Milly," he teased.

"Well, I feel quite flattered. Milly's going to play a big part in your life, Kevin. That's a very special friendship you have with her and you must treasure it. Now then," he went on in a business-like way, "do you feel like having another try?"

"Oh, yes, please," Kevin answered eagerly, "but I'd like to see the others again before I do."

"That's all right, but you mustn't take too long. Time in the real world is short."

Edgar, Megara and Jules came strolling along by the side of the stream. Megara's arms were full of wild iris and Jules was leading Pit by a grass rope he'd made himself. Edgar was doing his best to look unconcerned, with a straw hanging out of the side of his mouth. He was sorry to be losing Kevin so soon. "I hear you're off again," he said gruffly.

"Yes," his friend answered. "I want to have another try at being Kevin."

Jules thought Kevin was very adventurous. "I almost wish I could come too," he said wistfully, "but I don't think I'm quite ready yet." Poor Jules was seldom quite ready for anything.

Megara was upset. There was a special bond between herself and Kevin and they both knew it. Saying goodbye wasn't easy. And yet, in a way, it wouldn't be goodbye because Milly would be there when Kevin returned. The boy surprised himself and everyone else by putting his arms around the girl and kissing her gently on the cheek. "That's to make up for my meanness when I was Darius," he told her.

Uncle Gregory cleared his throat. An unexpected lump had formed there and after a few loud *harrumphs* he took Kevin by the arm and led him to where the Old Stone Bridge crossed the stream.

"Off you go then," he said, giving the boy a little push, "back the way you came."

Kevin ran over the bridge and turned once to see Uncle Gregory standing on the opposite bank. He was shouting, "And learn to ride that pony this time!"

"Don't worry, I will," Kevin called back. "Look after Pit for me."

As he ran forward into the mist he felt himself becoming smaller and smaller until he was no more than a pinpoint of light.

13
The Power of Thought

Milly had been restless all day. In school her thoughts constantly turned to Kevin and she could hardly wait for class to finish so that she could hurry to the hospital.

Kevin had been in a deep coma for two months now and there had been little to encourage the doctor to think that he might regain consciousness soon.

His parents were putting on a brave face, but as the weeks went by they became despondent. "He seems to be getting further and further away from us every day," his mother said. His father had given up reading to the unconscious boy—it hardly seemed worth it, somehow. He just sat by the bed, looking sadly at his son and wishing with all his heart that the terrible accident had never happened. "Why did it have to be Kevin?" he kept asking.

The only person who had never for a moment lost faith was Milly. She was absolutely certain that Kevin was *around*, as she described it to herself. "I don't know where he is, but I do know he isn't just lying there like a sack of potatoes doing nothing," she murmured.

"What did you say?" her teacher asked, seeing Milly's lips moving.

"Nothing, Miss Osborne," Milly answered quickly. "I was just thinking out loud." She could hardly have tried to explain; it would sound ridiculous.

When the school bell rang at the end of the final class of the day Milly took off like a greyhound. She even left her jacket behind her in her haste to get away.

Running most of the way to the hospital, she was filled with a strange sense of urgency.

"I must get there in time," she kept panting, without knowing exactly why.

Kevin's mother was by his bed and looked up as Milly came pounding through the door. "Goodness, Child," she exclaimed, "You're early today!"

"I ran all the way," Milly puffed. "I felt that perhaps Kevin might have woken up."

"I'm sorry, Dear," his mother said gently. "I'm afraid nothing's changed. But here," she rose from her chair by the bed, "sit down and get your breath. I'm going now and someone will be along to relieve you in a couple of hours." As she left the hospital room, she turned and whispered, "Thank you, Milly. You don't know what a help you are."

The hospital was quiet at this time of the afternoon. Kevin lay like a waxen image; the only improvement in his appearance over the weeks had been a slight, rosy flush in his cheeks.

Milly leaned towards him, her chin on her hands. "Oh, wherever you are, Kevin," she thought fiercely, "come back to us."

As if in answer to her plea, he gave a little cry—so soft it was, more like a kitten mewing than anything else. Then suddenly, his eyes flew open and he looked straight at Milly, who was so startled she gasped. "Megara," he murmured, and closed his eyes again.

Milly could have cried with disappointment. "Kevin," she begged again, "don't go away! Please stay here!" Minutes went by. Then, once more his eyes opened, but this time more slowly, fluttering as though the lids were heavy. Gradually focusing on his friend's face, he breathed, "Milly, it's you!" and stayed awake.

Her eyes ablaze with joy, Milly squeezed his hand, then raced off down the corridor to fetch a nurse. "He's awake! He's awake!" she shouted, completely forgetting that one should be quiet in a hospital. But the excitement was too great. The nurses on Kevin's ward had made him their special patient and they longed to see the little boy regain consciousness. Now, those who were on duty pelted back along the corridor with Milly to find him looking curiously around the room.

"Where am I this time?" he asked wonderingly.

"You're back again," Milly said triumphantly, giving him an awkward hug.

"Back home?" Kevin queried. Seeing Milly nod emphatically, he gave a huge, happy sigh and fell into the first natural sleep he'd had since the accident.

His parents, overjoyed at the news that their son had regained consciousness, hurried to his bedside to wait for Kevin to wake naturally. It wasn't long before he gave a yawn, stretched and, smiling a brilliant smile, reached out his arms to his mom and dad.

They found his first words puzzling. "Oh, I'm so glad I've been given another chance to be Kevin," he said.

Milly, who had stayed behind to wait with Kevin's parents, thought to herself, "There's something strange about all this," but as usual she kept her thoughts to herself.

Kevin remained in hospital for another week and Milly got special permission to take a day off school to keep him company.

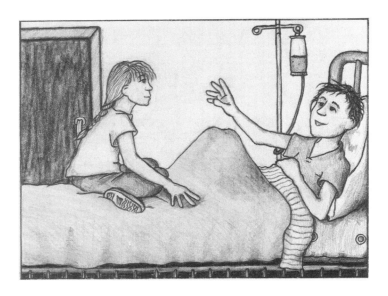

When they were alone together she asked
him, "What did you mean when you said you
were glad to be having another chance to be
Kevin?"

Her friend looked solemn. "I don't think I
can tell anyone about this except you," he
said. "I was in a sort of in between place where
you learn all kinds of new things that you can
bring back here. Sometimes you don't always
come back as yourself, but as someone else. I
didn't want to do that so I was allowed to
come back as me."

Milly nodded thoughtfully. She was good at accepting strange ideas. "Do you think you were in a *real* place," she asked, "or were you just dreaming while you were unconscious?"

"Honestly, I don't know," Kevin said worriedly. "I'd love to think it was real. It *seemed* real—but then all dreams do while you're dreaming them. And now I'm back it's beginning to fade. Uncle Gregory was there. I'm sure he was real." He looked at Milly shyly. "And by the way, so were you!"

"I was?" she asked, mystified.

"Yes, it was you and *not* you. In fact, your name was Megara, not Milly."

"Why, that's what you called me when you first opened your eyes," the girl exclaimed. "You looked right at me and said, 'Megara,' and then went off again."

"I don't think I'll ever be able to describe it all," Kevin sighed. "I wonder, did you have any odd dreams while I was gone?"

"Oh yes," Milly cried, as she remembered her dreams of walking and talking with Kevin. "Of course I did! How could I forget? We were on a beautiful beach and you had a shaggy pony with you that you were crazy about."

Kevin sat up. "That proves it," he said firmly. "It must have been real, because the pony was with me nearly all the time I was away."

The two youngsters spent most of the day trying to sort out the strange experience Kevin had been through. Some of it was very bewildering, some of it made a lot of sense, and all of it was fascinating. But they kept it to themselves, feeling that it was much too unusual to discuss with grownups. "You know how practical they are," Milly reminded her friend.

"There's one thing I'm sure I'll never forget," Kevin said, "and that's the video I saw." He told Milly, as best he could, of the wonderful dream that had come to him—of how all things are linked together and dependent on each other. His explanation was fumbled and more than a bit muddled, but Milly listened patiently.

Then it all became too much for her. Jumping up from her chair she whirled happily around the room, flinging her arms wide. "I don't care if what happened was only a dream or really true. I'm just glad that you're here and that we're going to be able to do so many exciting things together again."

By now, Kevin was feeling tired. He snuggled down into the pillows and Milly, sensing his weariness, slipped quietly from the room.

For her, this day had been a revelation. There was so much to think about, so much to try and understand. She sighed. Maybe it was time to get back to normal living again and just let these strange happenings take a back seat for a while.

Kevin's eleventh birthday was coming up soon and he would be home for the big day. When his parents asked him what he wanted most of all, he said immediately, "Please can I have riding lessons when I'm better?"

Milly burst out laughing. "Oh, really," she said, "I knew that's what you'd ask for!"

In Kevin's in between world, Pit the pony galloped joyfully around the fields by the Old Stone Bridge, knowing that the next time they met he'd be able to give the boy the ride of his life.